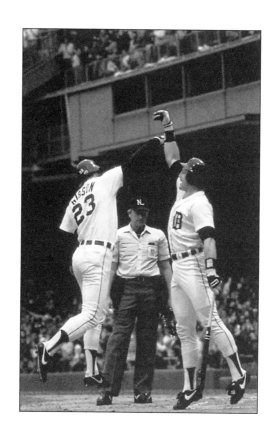

D
E
T
R
O
I
T

RICHARD RAMBECK

THE HISTORY OF THE
TIGERS

CREATIVE EDUCATION

Published by Creative Education
123 South Broad Street, Mankato, Minnesota 56001
Creative Education is an imprint of The Creative Company

Designed by Rita Marshall
Editorial assistance by Julie Bach & John Nichols

Photos by: Allsport Photography, Focus on Sports, SportsChrome.

Library of Congress Cataloging-in-Publication Data

Rambeck, Richard.
The History of the Detroit Tigers / by Richard Rambeck.
p. cm. — (Baseball)
Summary: A team history of the Detroit Tigers, who gave us Ty Cobb,
Al Kaline, and nearly a century of memories.
ISBN: 0-88682-908-9

1. Detroit Tigers (Baseball team)—History—Juvenile literature.
[1. Detroit Tigers (Baseball team)—History. 2. Baseball—History.]
I. Title. II. Series: Baseball (Mankato, Minn.)

GV875.D6R355   1999
796.357'64'0977434—dc21   97-7134

First edition

9 8 7 6 5 4 3 2 1

It's hard to believe that the sprawling, bustling metropolis of Detroit, Michigan, started out more than 250 years ago as a small frontier fort. The outpost was located on a plot of land that connected two of the Great Lakes—Huron and Erie, and its location made it ideal for trading. In the War of 1812, British and American forces battled fiercely for control of the growing village, because whoever possessed Detroit would have access to the waterways best suited for trade and transportation.

By the 1900s, Detroit grew to depend on another type of transportation: the automobile. The city became the automo-

The sweet swing of Ty Cobb.

1 9 0 1

The Tigers played their first season in the new AL, finishing third under manager George Stallings.

bile manufacturing center of the world. Cars and trucks have always been big business in America, but Detroit's leading role in the industry helped it become known the world over as the "Motor City."

Detroit is still a major international trading port. Goods are shipped to and from the city, through the Great Lakes, and up the St. Lawrence Seaway. Detroit is also served by 10 railroads and several airlines.

Indeed, the people of Detroit have a lot to be proud of, but one of their biggest sources of pride involves the city's rich sports history. The oldest professional team in Detroit is the major league baseball club, the Detroit Tigers. When the American League was formed in 1901, Detroit was granted a franchise. Nearly 100 years later, the team is still running strong. Young stars like Tony Clark and Bobby Higginson are keeping the Tigers of today on the prowl, but even in the 1900s the club was a success, finishing third in its inaugural season.

The Tigers placed third again in 1905, the year an 18-year-old outfielder named Tyrus Raymond Cobb joined the team. Cobb would stay with the club for 22 years and would establish a standard for hitting that may never be equaled.

COBB LEAVES OPPONENTS FIT TO BE TIED

On his first trip to the plate as a Tiger, in a game against the New York Highlanders (later named the New York Yankees), Cobb slammed a run-scoring double against Jack Chesbro, a pitcher who had won 41 games the season before. That was the first of 4,191 hits that Cobb would have in

A star for the 21st century, Tony Clark.

his major-league career, a record that stood until Pete Rose broke it in 1985.

Cobb batted only .240 his first year, but that was the only time his average was under .300. In 13 years he won 12 American League batting titles, including nine in a row from 1907 to 1915. In 1911 and 1912 he hit more than .400. During his early years with the Tigers, the team was a consistent pennant winner or contender. In fact, the Tigers won the American League pennant three years in a row, from 1907 to 1909. Detroit fans were disappointed, though, when their team lost the World Series every one of those years.

Still, Detroit was an exciting team, and Cobb was known as the best hitter in baseball. But opponents and some sportswriters believed he was also a dirty player. They accused Cobb of sharpening the spikes on his baseball shoes and then going out of his way to try to gore the opposition when he slid into bases. Cobb denied this. "It is untrue. At no time did I use a file or any other sharpening device."

The man known as the "Georgia Peach" had ability that was matched only by his confidence. Once, in the late 1950s, a sportswriter asked Cobb what his batting average would be if he were hitting against modern pitching. Cobb paused, thought for a moment and said, "I think I'd probably hit about .270 or .280." The reporter was shocked at the modest response from the lifetime .367 hitter. "Why so low Mr. Cobb?" inquired the reporter. "Are pitchers nowadays that much better?" Cobb laughed, looked at the stunned reporter and said, "No, son, I'd hit .280 today because I'm 70 years old."

1 9 1 1

The legendary Ty Cobb established a Tigers record by hitting safely in 40 consecutive games.

Cobb was a remarkable player, but his hard-driving personality caused both teammates and opponents to dislike him. "Ty Cobb is a low-down, miserable excuse for a human being," grumbled teammate Sam Crawford. "He's also the greatest player I've ever seen." Many people in baseball agreed, and in 1936, Cobb became the first player to be inducted into the baseball Hall of Fame.

For several years during Cobb's career with the Tigers, he, Crawford, and Bobby Veach keyed the Detroit attack. No matter how hard they tried, however, they couldn't produce a World Series title. Cobb also managed the Tigers for eight seasons. By the time he retired in 1926, the Tigers had fallen on hard times. For seven years after Cobb left, they finished no higher than fourth in the American League. These years were also hard for the team's fans. Many of them had lost their fortunes and their jobs in the Great Depression. With no extra money in their pockets, they stopped coming to Detroit home games. Attendance hit an all-time low in 1933. Things looked bleak for the Tigers—and for the nation. At that point, it was hard to believe that success for the team was only a year away, but it was, due to a catcher named Mickey Cochrane.

Cochrane was sold to the Tigers by the Philadelphia Athletics after the dismal 1933 season. The price tag was $100,000—a fortune in those days—but Cochrane proved to be worth every penny. He was not only a first-rate catcher, but also the team manager. Under his direction, almost all of Detroit's top hitters improved in 1934. Hank Greenberg shed his image as an awkward, lumbering giant and batted .339

1 9 3 4

For the second year in a row, Charlie Gehringer was selected as a starter in the All-Star Game.

A star of the '60s, Denny McLain.

Lou Whitaker, a standout 20 years later.

Hank Greenberg was named the AL MVP after leading the league with 39 homers and 170 RBIs.

with 139 RBIs. Charlie Gehringer hit .356; Marv Owen, .317; Jo-Jo White, .313; and Goose Goslin, .305. Cochrane himself hit .320.

Meanwhile, the pitching staff took an upswing as well. It was led by Lynwood "Schoolboy" Rowe, who had been only 7–4 in 1933. In 1934, he compiled an impressive 24–8 record and won 16 games in a row. Tommy Bridges made the same dramatic improvement, at 14–12 in 1933 and 22–11 in 1934.

In spite of the Depression, the Detroit fans flocked to see the reborn Tigers. In 1934, the Tigers won their first American League pennant in 25 years. Attendance almost tripled, to nearly one million, as the Tigers finished the season with a record of 101–53. But then, the same old curse descended on the team. They lost the World Series to the St. Louis Cardinals four games to three. It seemed they would never enjoy the status of being the best in baseball.

The following year, the Tigers staggered out of the gate and by May were in last place. But the team rallied, led by Hank Greenberg, who had 36 homers, 170 RBIs, and a .328 average—enough to win the American League Most Valuable Player award. The Tigers eventually overtook the powerful New York Yankees to win another pennant, but the question remained—could they finally win the World Series? The Tigers put their unsuccessful history behind them and beat the Chicago Cubs four games to two. After 35 years of pro baseball, the city of Detroit finally had its first World Series winner.

For several years, the Tigers remained one of the top teams in baseball. They owed their success largely to Cochrane and Greenberg, along with Rowe and Bridges. Unfortunately, Cochrane had to retire after being hit by a pitch in 1938. Greenberg stepped in to become the team's inspirational leader. That same year, he threatened to break Babe Ruth's single-season home-run record. The Detroit slugger slammed 58, only two off of Ruth's 1927 mark of 60.

In 1940, Greenberg was again named the American League Most Valuable Player. That year he led the Tigers to another American League pennant. Five years later they won the pennant again, and for the second time in club history they claimed the World Series title. Coincidentally, they beat the Chicago Cubs again, four games to two.

After 10 years of solid play sprinkled with four pennants and two World Series titles, the Detroit fans would have to wait more than 20 years for the Tigers' next championship team. Greenberg, Gehringer, Rowe, and Bridges retired during these years, and the team began losing consistently. But the Tigers still had a few talented players—especially third baseman George Kell, who won the 1949 AL batting title, and pitcher Hal Newhouser, who retired in 1953 with 200 career victories.

July 20: Detroit hurler Jim Bunning pitched a no-hitter in defeating Boston, 3–0.

KALINE MAKES BEELINE FOR GREATNESS

The year Newhouser left the Detroit Tigers, an upstart 18-year-old outfielder named Al Kaline joined the team. Kaline went straight from high school to the majors, never playing an inning of minor-league ball. When he joined the Tigers in 1953, the youthful Kaline knew nothing about the major leagues. He was scared and in awe of everything around him, especially manager Fred Hutchinson, a gruff,

Outfielder Willie Horton led the Tigers with a .285 average and 36 home runs.

intimidating man. But Hutchinson took a particular interest in the young rookie and told him to watch and learn as much as he could.

At first Kaline served as a defensive replacement in the late innings. Although he played little, he expected nothing less than perfection from himself. In the ninth inning of one game, Kaline raced after a line drive and then dove, but he didn't catch the ball. The opposition scored two runs on the play, and the Tigers lost the game. Afterward, Kaline was upset. "I thought I should have caught it because I was used to catching everything on the sandlots," he later recalled. "But they hit the ball a lot sharper in the major leagues, and I just couldn't reach the ball this time." Kaline remembered how pitcher Ted Gray tried to console him. "Don't worry about it," he told Kaline. "You made a great effort. A lot of guys wouldn't have even tried for the ball."

That kind of effort characterized Kaline's career. He had hustle, and he was also an outstanding hitter. In 1955, when he was only 20 years old, he won the American League batting title, making him the youngest player ever to lead either league in hitting. But Kaline didn't have much help from the rest of the Detroit lineup. During the 1950s, the Tigers' hitting attack consisted mostly of Kaline and outfielder Harvey Kuenn. Soon, however, the "K" boys would have reinforcements.

In 1960, Norm Cash, a first baseman, joined the team. He won the American League batting title a year later with a .361 average. Then catcher Bill Freehan became a Tiger in 1961. In 1963, the Detroit roster was improved further by the additions of slugging outfielder Willie Horton and pitchers

All-Star infielder Cecil Fielder.

World Series MVP, pitcher Mickey Lolich.

Mickey Lolich and Denny McLain. Utility player Mickey Stanley arrived the following year.

For the first time in a long time, the Tigers had the talent of a championship team, but bad luck still haunted them. They nearly won the 1967 American League pennant, but faded near the end of the season. Many people in baseball felt bad for Kaline, who'd been with the Tigers for 15 years and had never played in a World Series.

Mark Fidyrch became only the second rookie pitcher in history to start in an All-Star Game.

Finally, in 1968, talent and good luck came together. Despite several key injuries, the team jumped to the top of the American League. One of the injuries was suffered by Kaline, who would miss much of the season. The Tigers still remained in first place, however, largely due to the amazing pitching of Denny McLain, who became the first major-league pitcher in 34 years to win 30 games, a feat no major-leaguer has accomplished since.

McLain earned both the Cy Young and the Most Valuable Player awards in the American League, but he wasn't the only Tiger who had a great year in 1968. Willie Horton slugged 36 home runs, Norm Cash and Bill Freehan each had 25, and outfielder Jim Northrup had 21. Freehan and outfielder Mickey Stanley, who didn't make a single error in center field all season, both won Gold Glove awards.

Due to these heroics, the Tigers won 103 games, a franchise record, to claim their first pennant in 23 years. This time they faced the St. Louis Cardinals in the World Series. The Tigers fell behind three games to one but rallied to win game five behind Mickey Lolich, who won his second game of the series, and Kaline, who drove in the winning run in a 5–3 victory. McLain won game six, setting up a decisive

Six-time AL All-Star, shortstop Alan Trammell (pages 18–19).

showdown in game seven with Lolich going against the Cardinals' ace Bob Gibson in St. Louis. Lolich pitched a masterful game, beating the Cardinals 4–1. He became the 12th pitcher in baseball history to win three games in a World Series. "I guess I'm an unlikely hero," Lolich said.

Kaline also was an unlikely hero. Hurt much of the season, he started in the series only because Detroit manager Mayo Smith had shuffled his lineup, moving Northrup from right field to center field, and Stanley from center to shortstop. This switch allowed Kaline to play right field. He responded by batting .379 with 11 hits and eight RBIs during the series.

Kaline played six more years for the Tigers, retiring after the 1974 season with 3,007 hits, 399 homers, and a lifetime

Lou Whitaker, whose Tigers career would span 18 years, was named Detroit's Rookie of the Year.

Powerful right fielder Kirk Gibson.

batting average of .297. His retirement marked the beginning of a down period for the Tigers. Fortunately, pitcher Mark "The Bird" Fidrych provided some much-needed thrills for Detroit fans in the late 1970s with his antics on the mound. He talked to the baseball and personally congratulated his teammates for good plays. But arm troubles prematurely ended his career. By 1979, the Tigers had a new manager, George "Sparky" Anderson, who had built the fabulous Cincinnati Reds teams of the 1970s. They also had a new set of stars, the best of whom was a pitcher named Jack Morris.

Sparky Anderson became the first manager to win the World Series in both the AL and NL.

MORRIS MASTERS THE FORKBALL

During the early 1980s, perhaps no pitcher in baseball was as dominant as Detroit right-hander Jack Morris. An occasionally hotheaded competitor, Morris wouldn't settle for second best. "Jack has such high expectations of himself that when he doesn't live up to them, he shows it—in public," said Detroit pitching coach Roger Craig.

Craig spent a lot of time with Morris and taught him the pitch that made him one of the best in baseball—the forkball. A forkball is thrown with the same motion as a fastball, but because the index and middle fingers are spread out when the pitcher grips the ball, the pitch drops just as it reaches the batter. To a batter, a well-thrown forkball looks as if the bottom falls out of it. Few pitchers have mastered the forkball the way Morris did. "He always was an outstanding pitcher with the fastball," said Tom Paciorek of the Chicago White Sox. "With the forkball, he's a great pitcher."

And in 1984, no team in baseball was as talented as the

Tigers ace Jack Morris.

Detroit Tigers. The team won 35 of its first 40 games. Morris won 10 of his first 11 decisions, including a no-hitter against the Chicago White Sox, the first thrown by a Detroit pitcher in 26 years. But Morris wasn't even the best pitcher on the Detroit staff that year. Relief pitcher Guillermo "Willie" Hernandez posted 32 saves and won both the Cy Young Award and MVP honors in the American League. Other players on the team helped to make it an impressive year. Catcher Lance Parrish had 33 homers and 98 RBIs, and right fielder Kirk Gibson hit 27 home runs and had 91 RBIs.

Led by these performances, the Tigers were in first place in the American League East every day of the 1984 season, finishing with a 104–58 record. They then swept the Kansas City Royals in the American League Championship Series and defeated the San Diego Padres four games to one to claim their first World Series title since 1968, with MVP honors going to shortstop Alan Trammell.

1 9 8 7

Catcher Matt Nokes played in the All-Star Game and was the AL Rookie of the Year.

TRAMMELL AND WHITAKER SPARK TIGERS

When it comes to double-play combinations, nobody did it better or longer than Alan Trammell and Lou Whitaker. The two stars set the American League record in 1995 with 1,918 appearances together as teammates. They also own the record for being the longest-lived double-play combination in major league history, turning two for the Tigers from 1977 to 1995. The twosome captured a combined six Gold Glove awards for fielding excellence, but they didn't just play the field; they both did heavy damage at the plate as well. Trammell and Whitaker combined for more than 400 homers and 2,000 RBIs during their careers, numbers unmatched by any other combination in history. "Those guys are incredible," remarked manager Sparky Anderson. "There's never been a twosome like them before, and for my money, I don't think you'll see anybody as good ever again."

Trammell, Whitaker, and the Tigers proved to be good enough in 1987 to capture another American League East title. Detroit was in second place behind the Toronto Blue Jays during the final weeks of the season, but led by Trammell, Whitaker, catcher Matt Nokes, and pitchers Jack Morris and Doyle Alexander, the Tigers caught the Blue Jays and won the division title. Although Detroit went on to lose to the Minnesota Twins in the American League Championship Series, it was a remarkable individual year for Trammell. He hit .343

First baseman Cecil Fielder led the American League with 51 home runs and 132 RBIs.

Tigers save leader, Mike Henneman.

with 28 homers and 105 RBIs, finishing second in the voting for league MVP.

After a second-place finish in 1988, the Tigers slumped miserably to last place in 1989. As the club prepared for a new decade, manager Sparky Anderson knew he needed to unearth some fresh talent. But when Detroit signed a little-known first baseman named Cecil Fielder, nobody paid much attention. After all, Fielder had failed to crack the Toronto Blue Jays' lineup while there from 1985 to 1988, and by '89 he found himself out of the majors, playing in Japan. "When I went over to Japan, I didn't expect to come back for a long time," Fielder said. But after hitting 38 homers for the Hanshin Tigers in 1989, Fielder got the chance to start over in Detroit.

On July 28 against the New York Yankees, Travis Fryman became the eighth Tiger in history to hit for the cycle.

The man known to his fans as "Big Daddy" immediately began to repay the Tigers for their confidence, rocketing to the top of the home run charts. "Everybody knew he had the power," said Gord Ash, Toronto's assistant general manager. "The question was how much was he going to play. Cecil struck us as the type of player who could achieve his maximum potential with everyday play. But we couldn't give him that." The Tigers could, however, and Fielder responded by leading the American League with 51 homers. It was the first time any player had reached 50 homers since George Foster hit 52 for the Cincinnati Reds in 1977.

Under Sparky Anderson's leadership, the Tigers picked up other quality players such as center fielder Lloyd Moseby from Toronto, outfielder and designated hitter Larry Sheets from Baltimore, and pitcher Dan Petry from California. Detroit's personnel moves paid off as the team rose from

Outfielder Bobby Higginson, an emerging star (pages 26–27).

Damion Easley came to Detroit in a July 31 trade with the Angels, then raised his season average from .156 to .268.

embarrassment in 1989 to respectability in 1991. The Tigers stayed in contention through mid-September and finished the season in a tie for second place.

Then, over the next four years, they enjoyed only one winning season, an 84–78 record in 1993. The players and managers realized they were still in a period of rebuilding through scouting and player development. The baseball strike of 1994 interrupted the team's efforts and cast a shadow over professional baseball.

A NEW STADIUM AND NEW PLAYERS

In 1995, the Tigers hired a new general manager, Randy Smith, who engineered a plan for retooling the major- and minor-league teams. At the same time, Tiger owner Mike Il-itch began pitching proposals for a new downtown stadium. The city of Detroit accepted his idea, and the new stadium was scheduled to open in 1999 in a sports complex that would include a domed stadium for Detroit's pro football team, the Lions.

News of the stadium didn't help the Tigers much in 1995. They finished with a record of 60–84. In the off-season, the Tigers hired new manager Buddy Bell. A veteran of 18 major league seasons as a player, Bell was hired for his base-ball experience and for his good nature and patience—traits that come in handy while developing young talent—and Bell had plenty of star material to work with. Youngsters like Tony Clark, Bobby Higginson, and Brian Hunter look to form the core of Detroit's next great team.

At 6-foot-7 and 245 pounds, Clark has a strong body and

sweet power stroke that has Tigers fans thinking big, in more ways than one. Clark bashed 27 homers in 1996, and followed it up with a 32-homer, 117-RBI performance in 1997. The former college basketball star has convinced his manager that first base is well taken care of for the Tigers. "Tony's just such a great athlete," said Bell. "He's barely scratched the surface of his ability, and that's scary."

Outfielder Bobby Higginson gives the Tigers another power threat to build their future. A solid fielder with a cannon arm, Higginson can play all three outfield positions, but the 27-year-old slugger makes his biggest impact at the plate. He hit .320 with 26 homers and 81 RBIs in 1996, and then followed it up with a .299 campaign with 27 homers and 101 RBIs the following season.

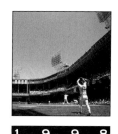

Historic Tiger Stadium closed its doors after 86 years as home to the Detroit team.

Young ace Justin Thompson.

Brian Hunter, AL stolen-base champion.

Gritty closer Todd Jones.

Brian Hunter provides raw speed at the top of the lineup and a steady glove in center field. The Portland, Oregon, native has improved steadily at the plate during his career and is already one of baseball's best base-stealers. Hunter hit .269 in 1997, scoring a phenomenal 112 runs, while swiping a league-high 74 bases.

The Tigers' offense also includes such veteran stalwarts as infielders Bip Roberts and Damion Easley, but for Detroit to make a pennant run, pitching will be the key. Youngsters like Justin Thompson and Brian Moehler will have keep improving, while veteran closer Todd Jones needs to maintain his high level of performance.

With a galaxy of young stars on the rise, and an organization fiercely commited to success, the Tigers have a new winning attitude to match their new home.